Dotty Ditties

loosely written verse

by Elizabeth Rose

Published in the United States by
Quillrunner Publishing LLC
Albuquerque, New Mexico

Printed in the U.S.A.

ISBN 978-0-9851157-2-2

To all grandchildren
—especially MINE

PIPOL TREE

In India they have a pipol tree
It must be the strangest of sights to see
Is it a bit like a person sort of leafy and tall
Or a bit like a strong man lifting them all

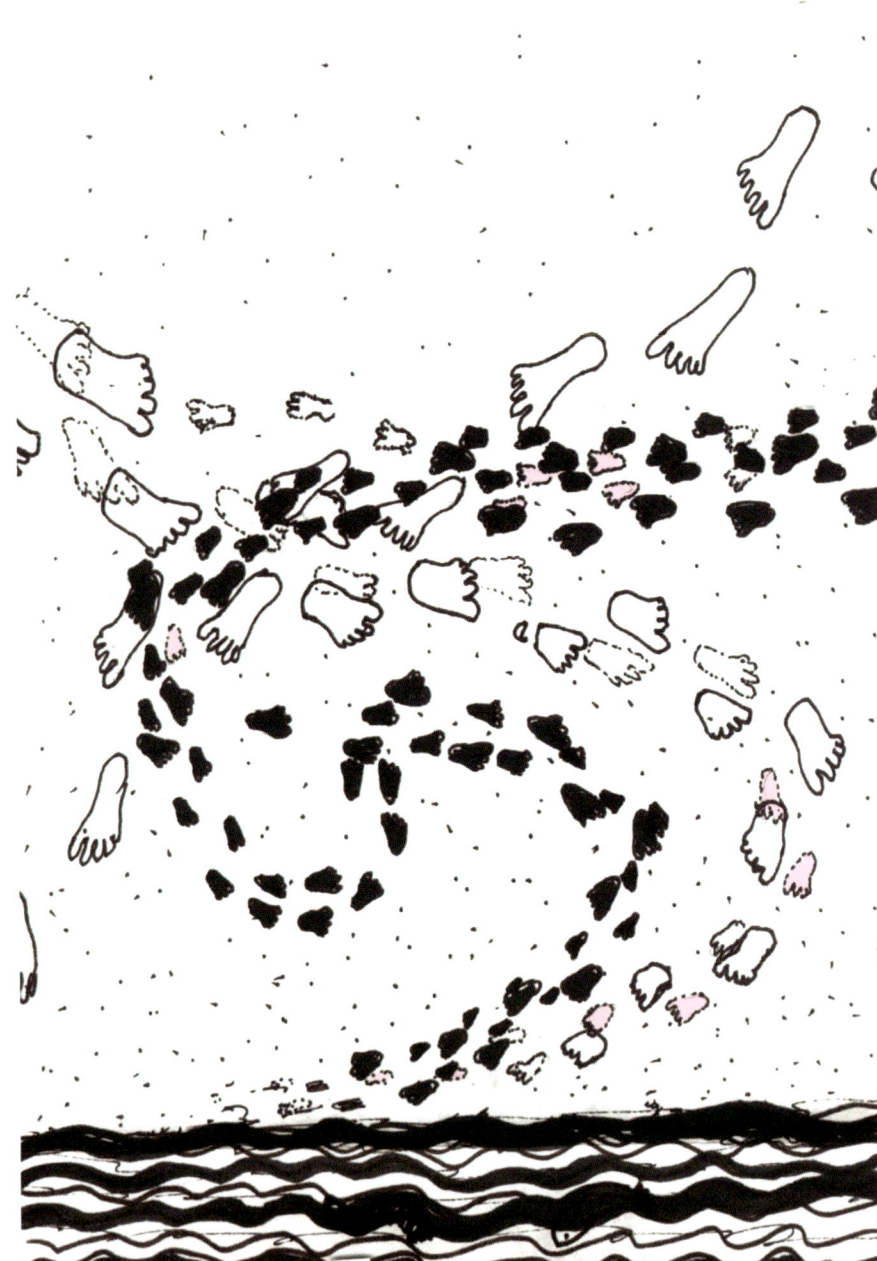

FOOTPRINTS

Following footprints in the sand
I wonder whom I walk behind
Some prints are so wide with toes so long
Some very faint and others strong
Jumping great steps to match their stride
I try to fit mine right inside
Turtles leave tracks
You do too
Do you know which ones belong to you

PARROTS SECRET

Parrots green
Beaks so red
Fly through the trees right past my head

Sometimes they stop to talk and shout
To nuzzle up and prance about
They must tell each other where they are going
But I don't have a way of knowing
With lots more squawks
Off they go
But where they go
I will never know

SILLY BILLY

Silly Billy was so daft
He thought the table was a raft
With fork and spoon
Rowed across the room
Stood on a chair
And laughed and laughed

TOUGH EGGS

If I was Humpty Dumpty and was sitting on a wall
And somebody was mean to me
And made me have a fall
I'd rub the hurt
Get right up
Then bravely march along
With all the soldiers and Kings men
And sing a cheerful song

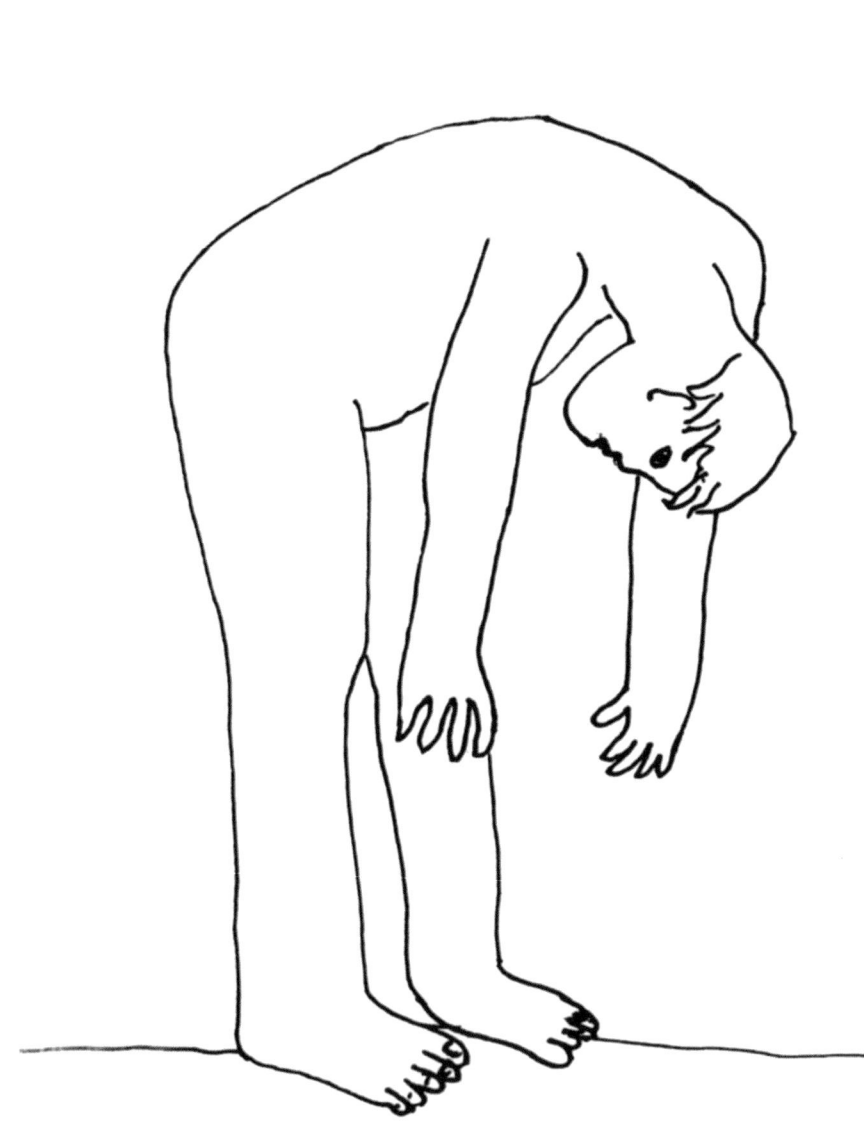

SKIN

I'm ever so glad I'm covered with skin
But how I wonder did I ever get in
It fits so snug
It fits so tight
With not even a button
Nor zipper in sight

ALI THE GATOR

Ali the gator loved being a waiter
The trouble was
Guests went hungry
Because…
Whatever they ate
Ali cleaned up their plates
Especially if…
Guests chose fish
Ali's most favorite
Favorite
Favorite dish

PANDA'S LUNCH

My jungle house is all bamboo
The bed the chair the table too
Bamboo poles make up the door
The walls the rafters roof and floor

One day I fear I'll hear a crunch
Crunching teeth
and
munch
munch
munch
Because uninvited Panda's dropping by
To eat my house up for his lunch

LEGS

Dogs need FOUR legs to keep upright
Unlike spiders who need EIGHT
Tables have FOUR though three would do
Birds and us people have just TWO
Flowers and trees can stand straight on ONE
But snakes and worms have exactly NONE

SHOAT

It's hard to tell a sheep from a goat
Both have four legs and a woolly coat
Billy
Nanny
Ewe and Ram
Two make a kid
Two make a lamb
Unless you can tell which one is which
A mistake could cost you
A toss in the ditch

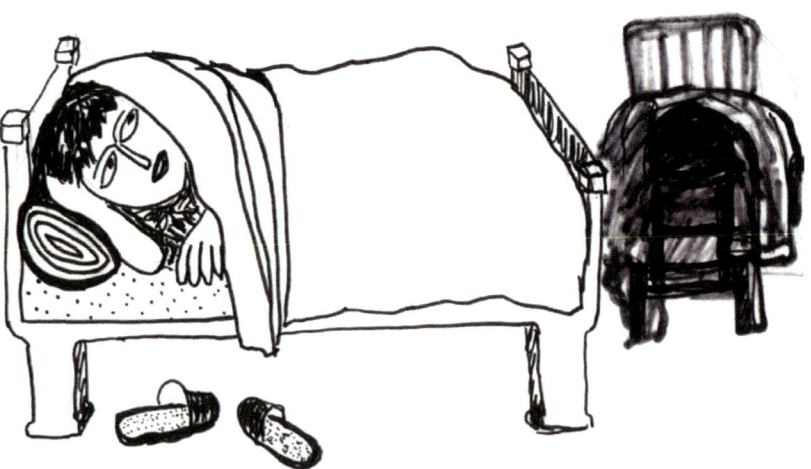

COCK A DOODLE DO

Cock a doodle do
Do get up
Rooster crows to us each day

Cock a doodle
DO SHUT UP
It's sleep–in time today

PRETTY POLLY

Pretty Polly Pretty Polly
Is a parrot's favorite ditty
Who was Polly I want to know
And was Polly really pretty

Polly put the kettle on
So we could all have tea
She roasted peanuts for the parrot
Baked currant buns for me

WAY TO THE SKY

At the top of the palm trees
Where nobody sees
There is a spike that sticks up
Above the top leaves
What is it there for
I want to know why
Is it showing the tree
The way to the sky

WISE OWL

Wise owl wise owl
Are you called wise
Because you have such enormous round eyes
Or is it the WIT within your tWITwoooooo
That makes a clever bird of you

HICKORY DICKORY...

Hickory Dickory Dock
The old mouse scampered up the clock
When the clock struck one
He had such a fright
He shivered and shook for the rest of the night

A-SLEEPING WITH THE FISHES

The sea keeps coming all night long
Each wave a lullaby
Its own sweet song
As each wave breaks upon the shore
My heart joins in and sings once more
And as I do so I fall asleep
And swim with the fishes in the deep

CPSIA information can be obtained
at www.ICGtesting.com
Printed in the USA
LVIC01n0909241013
358347LV00001B/8

9780985115722